Praise for

UNFATHOMABLE AND OTHER POEMS

"This collection…captures and paints the landscape of vibrant memories and sombre shadows which have shaped identity, and invites readers to envisage how their sense of selves may be located in their lived experiences." —Diana Abrams lives in Toronto, Canada; her writing credits are in fields relating to academic discourses on transnational migration, identify and belonging.

"This tour de force of poetic memoir deserves a place on the book shelf of every person who knows that life can only be understood looking back, but must be lived in the present moment and in the future." — Raymond Holmes – Author of *Witnesses And Other Short Stories*

"Reading Unfathomable…One is aware of the sounds, smells and music of the country…using structure and sound to take the reader into the poem." —Jennifer Footman, author of *St. Valentine's Day*

"This collection of poems peels back the curtain on this remote corner of the world to reveal Guyana in all its beauty and ugliness. These poignant, emotionally satisfying and individualistic poems breathe life, and death, into the Guyanese experience." — Michael Joll, author of *Perfect Execution* and *Persons Of Interest*

OTHER BOOKS BY
KEN PUDDICOMBE

Racing With The Rain (2012)

Junta (2014)

Down Independence Boulevard And Other Stories (2017)

UNFATHOMABLE
And Other Poems

By

Ken Puddicombe

MiddleRoad | Publishers

www.middleroadpublishers.ca

Making Literature See The Light Of Day

Library and Archives Canada Cataloguing in Publication

ISBN 978-1-9991365-5-0 (softcover)

Cover photographs courtesy of:

Deep Blue Sea by Barun Patro

FreeBridge by L.M. Orek

Cover Design by Ken Puddicombe

UNFATHOMABLE AND OTHER POEMS

by Ken Puddicombe

"Tis looking back that gives the future colour,
Because, in life, we find
The past analogizes all the future
Upon the plastic mind…"

Egbert Martin, British Guianese Poet (1861-1890)

DEDICATION

To my wife Rohini and daughters Karen and Kathryn
who continue to provide inspiration.

And to Emma and Dana who will hopefully read this one
day in the near future.

ACKNOWLEDGMENT

These poems were inspired mainly by my first novel
Racing With The Rain and other notes written over many
years

TABLE OF CONTENTS

1. VISIONS

Eyes seeing long after lids are closed.

Images locked in the subconscious.

Streaks of light. Shadows.

Shapes clutter the

Landscape of

My vision.

They dangle. Dance.

Dart before my eyes.

Creatures haunt me. Faces

Don't go away. Places

I've been to. People

I've met. Things I have done.

Sleep takes time. Unfinished

tasks. Dreams of glory.

Visions of bygone

Days. Moments

Of elusive

Happiness. Unrealized hopes.

What if's...

2. I AM WHO I AM

I am from Guyana.

Once called British Guiana.

The Land Of Many Waters and

The towering Kaieteur.

I am the sum total of generations

Who came long before I took my first breath.

I am the product of east meets west.

The descendant of people from

Far-away lands who found

Their way to an unknown country,

Seeking a better life.

They came from England

And took over plantations from the Dutch.

They were overseers, part of the

White Plantocracy. The people who enforced

The Indentureship laws.

Saw that the sugar estate

Ran efficiently and made profits

For the absentee landlord in England
Sipping his tea sweetened with sugar
Made from cane grown in
British Guiana. Along with Demerara
Rum for the mighty English navy
Sailing the seven seas,
Ruling an empire where
The sun never set.

They also came from India and worked
The land for those white plantation owners
In England and Scotland. They grew the cane,
Cut it at harvest time, filled the punts,
Went home to their garden plots
To supplement their piece wage.

They were planters, cane cutters, stackers
Weeders. They worked in the fields
And in the factory. They lifted and heaved.
They walked with bundles
Balanced on their head.

And somewhere
Along the way a lineage was created
Including me along with many others.

*

They braved a long voyage across the sea.

They worked long hours in the blazing tropical sun.

They survived and built a home away from home.

I am the product of east meets west.

For better or worse, that's who I am.

I am grateful to the pioneers who left their homeland.

And I don't pass judgment.

 Because, if they hadn't come,

Where would I be, today?

3. UNFATHOMABLE

The slanting rays of the sinking sun
Set the slats of the jalousie windows aglow
Creating pools of darkness all around:
In front of the door to the portico,
Behind the coffee table in the gallery.
Below the cabinet in the dining room.

The kitchen door was ajar.
Through it floated strains
Of the wind rustling through
The mango tree in the front yard.

Voices came from afar.
Children laughing and playing,
Jeering and calling to me from the
Playground where I'd hurried home
After hearing the news of the death
Of my friend Lincoln.

My head grew larger with every
Passing minute. The hair on my scalp

And back of my neck bristled,

My eyes were ready to pop

In their sockets.

What was that odour

Clinging to me? In my nostrils,

The ever present, ever destructive

Smell of death. It followed

Me from the cemetery my mother

And I passed on our return trip

After visiting relatives.

All through that long walk, I had inhaled it.

A decaying, putrid, ever present stench

Lingering in the very air that I breathed.

Everything around me assumed unfathomable

Proportions. I was in a room with the ceiling

Inclined to meet the floor at the far end,

All the furniture piled up against one of the walls.

Shadows detached themselves from dark corners,

Assumed shapes of moving objects and taunted me.

Doors closed and opened. Through one of them

I had a vision of Lincoln…

*****

The mid-afternoon heat had risen
To stifling proportions.
Up and down both sides of the Punt Trench,
The vapour rose in pools floating slowly
Off the road, held there in a haze
Through which everything unfurled
In distorted segments.

The occasional burst
Of breeze stirring down the Punt Trench
Sent ripples through the reeds both sides
Of the parapet. Animals stood on the dirt
Road, panting and heaving.
People lazed around in hammocks
In bottom-houses and fanned themselves.
And the kids took refuge in the Punt Trench.

Lincoln was plunging
From the parapet. Then he was throwing
Somersaults, sending surges of water
Slapping against an unsuspecting victim.
Now, he was pulling someone's short-pants down,
Throwing it on to the roadside

Where the kid would have to retrieve

It, naked. Throughout this all,

Lincoln was laughing.

I remembered.

Once, not so long ago,

I had pushed him into the Punt Trench,

And ran away, laughing at my own audacity.

From up the road came the resounding

Echo of a whip cracking in the air

As a mule-train laden with cane stalks and

Molasses made its way westward.

The punts in the mule-train linked

With short lengths of chain hooked

Into metal clasps welded at the front

And rear of each craft. Six mules up front

Kept the convoy moving, each animal

Bound to a punt by a length of chain.

Lincoln was clinging to the connecting

Chain between two punts in the middle

Of the convoy, hanging on for a ride,

When the distance narrowed swiftly

Between the punts.

I saw those eyes, those cat-eyes

That could dazzle and awe. The shock

On Lincoln's face as he sensed

What was about to happen

As the punts closed in. His teeth clenched.

His bones crushed mercilessly

As the water turned crimson.

***

I remembered my parents coming home.

My mother rubbed me down with *Limachol*

And mentholated spirits, my father

Reassuring me everything would be fine.

The alcohol-based balm cooled my head

And calmed my nerves, the voice of my

Father, composed and soothing,

Gave me hope that I would live,

I would not join Lincoln,

In his watery grave.

4. FALLING

I was falling.
Slowly. helplessly, down, down, down.
And there was nothing I could do.

The swirling waters of the Punt Trench
Below, the bridge above
Where I'd been sitting seconds before.

I wasn't sure how it happened:
Whether I'd jumped or been pushed,
But I knew I was falling.

Arms flailing, body catapulting
Into the brown, murky water
That would propel me towards
The koker, out to the gaping
Mouth of the Demerara River.

From there I'd be sucked into
The Atlantic, to wash up on
Some unknown beach or sink
To the bottom of the ocean.

I opened my mouth to shout

But words failed me.

If only I could grab hold of something

To break my fall, but there was nothing

 –just the bridge above, the water below.

I was terrified. Why didn't

Someone help me?

People passed over the bridge,

And yet, no one paid attention.

They seemed to deliberately

Ignore me, dooming me to my fate.

And still, I kept on falling, falling.

5. RACING WITH THE RAIN

The Punt Trench.
Our very own preserve
Where we idled away those long,
Endless summers.

Often, in the middle
Of the afternoon, white clouds
Billowing, sunshine rushing in waves
Along the road, a sudden stillness settled
Over surroundings.

From as far as the eye could see
Along a road narrowing to the outer fringes
Of the Backdam, the sky came alive with a familiar
Changing pattern.

First a light patter,
Nothing more than a slight
Disturbance, something more like
The gradual awakening at daybreak or the
Calm heralding sunset when parrots bed down

In the trees and gauldings wing their way to the
Botanical gardens.

Like the roll of distant
Drums gradually growing louder with
Every passing minute, finally rising to a crescendo,
It descended.

*

Playing in the Crossroad,
We grabbed our marbles and
Ran down Middle Road, the steady
Staccato beat at our heels, the sound
Amplified on zinc sheets as we tried to outrun
The eruption.

Almost home when overtaken by the swift
Moving dark cloud, heavy drops splattering and stinging.
Drenched to the skin by the time I arrived at my front gate,
Clothes clinging.

Up the stairs,
Safely inside. Trees
Bending, swaying, heaving.

Discarded leaves and debris caught

In a whirlpool. Moved along in frenzy across

The road, around the front yard, up the stairs,

To the landing, the cloud passed swiftly heading for the

Demerara River.

How exhilarating it all was.

In those days, we were always Racing with

The rain.

6. DROWNING

Up and down the Punt Trench

In the shimmering rays of the afternoon
Sun, light bouncing off the cocoa-brown surface
Of the water.

Silhouetted heads bobbing up and down.

I climbed the five steps. Took a seat.
Every time someone jumped
I found myself heaving on the bridge,

My small frame hanging precariously over the edge.

With every leap I tasted the water
On my lips. Felt the excitement
Of the jump.

Experienced the thrill of taking a plunge.

I hit the water with a resounding

Splash. Went down, into the deep,

Murky, swirling pit of the Punt Trench

Into regions I'd never imagined existed.

I groped around the depths.

Locked in a dark room, unable to see

Except for slivers of light created by

My memory of what it was like to wake up

Early in the morning and see

Sunlight seeping through the cracks of the wallboards.

Everything awash in liquid brown.

Why didn't someone come for me?

Surely they remembered I couldn't swim?

I came to the surface once,

Hands thrashing, trying to grab

Something. Anything.

If only I could make it to the parapet,

So close and yet so far.

I started on my way down

For the second time, images and bodies

In motion clouding my vision and

Confusing my mind. I was a kid

Lost in the Backdam, not knowing

Whether to wait for someone to find

Me or continue

My desperate act of wandering.

I sank to the bottom again. My feet touched

Mud and silt, adding to the murkiness.

I sensed my movement slowing. I held my lips tight.

Opened my eyes wide, trying to peer through

The brown liquid. Could see nothing

Beyond my hands, hear nothing but the

Gurgling water rushing past my ears.

I gasped and choked. Was I already

On the way to the Demerara River?

Then to the Atlantic?

Would I ever see my mother and father again?

When I thought there was no end,

Something took hold of my hand

And tugged me. I was a punt

Being hauled by a large mule. I clung

To it with all my might,

The first firm object I'd felt in an eternity.

I felt the movement, saw the rush of water

Going past me again. This time I was

Moving upwards, faster and faster,

To an area with light glowing

In all its glory. Light, like the break of day,

Light dazzling and

Brilliant like I'd never known existed.

I was lying on the parapet, looking

Up at faces blocking the sunlight and

Staring anxiously at me. I gasped, choked

And sputtered. I'd seen the cat do that

When she'd eaten the praying mantis

In the back yard. I was also sick to my stomach,

The portion of the Canal drunk

Coming up the same way entered.

The relief of being on firm ground
Again, nothing compared to it.

7. CALL IN THE NIGHT

A harsh vibration splinters
The stillness. If I ignore it
Will the sound go away?

Numbers emblazoned in red
Against a black background:
4:25.

The last digit slides into a cavity.
Another replaces it from
A limitless reservoir at the top.

An endless cycle of time.
Is this my life?
4:27.

Passages in time. Two minutes
have elapsed before my eyes:
120 seconds.

There has been no earth-shattering

Event unfolding in the world.
Nothing that has bearing on my life.

*

Lying there in bed dangling
In this zone between sleep and
Consciousness

I am overcome by a strange
Feeling. I am losing control.
4:29

The phone rings again.
An ungodly hour for someone
Trying to get hold of me.

A late Indian summer
Has given false hope
Of a delayed winter.

A sudden chill penetrates
Below the comforter, gets hold
Of my toes.

Slowly works its way up my ankles

To my calves. My fingers are numb.

I can't feel the phone.

Who is it that suffers the impact more?

The bearer of bad news

Or the one about to receive it?

8. GOING BACK

The long slanting rays
Of the sun bounced off the silver skin
Of the 747, pushing an ever-reluctant area
Of luminosity.

A dirt road ran parallel to a wide river. The road
Just a narrow swath — emptiness carved
Out of the woods.

The bright glow raced
Ahead of the plane, swerved
As it hit a crude wooden bridge, bounced
Off a cluster of rooftops, disappeared again as it passed
Over a stretch of trees.

The luminous disk hesitated, crept slowly
Into the nearby river, its mutable bulk undulating
with the waves. After entering It became a fiery
omelette, ever changing bands of orange,
Pink and maroon
Surrounding it.

Going back. Could one ever really go back?

Flying through a field of white clouds,

No reference point above or below, the silence

Broken only by the constant hum of the engine,

The plane buffeted by an air pocket.

That's how it always was in British Guiana

During the colonial days: periods of calm

When nothing happened and time stood

Still, and those intervals with events

Changing our lives forever.

Suddenly, we ran into

A rain cloud. Large drops

Poured down, bounced off the

Metal skin, cascaded down the flaps

And disappeared into the grey void below.

Droplets formed on the window, were caught

In the backward flow of an air stream created by

the movement of the plane, and dispersed into rivulets.

Sixteen years: More than a decade. One hundred and
ninety-two

Months. Not a very long period when considered in the

Passage of time, but long enough to warp the memory

And dull the senses, And like loosely connected

Parts of a puzzle, the years fall into place

Once the pieces

Are joined.

Going back. Could one ever really go back?

9. MIDDLE ROAD

Houses were dark shadows against the night sky,

Fast moving rain clouds precipitous and ominous.

An eerie silence pervaded the surroundings.

Instinct gave me clues to my whereabouts.

Memories of locations and names

Of places and people came flashing back.

At the Junction once was the Cake Shop.

Opposite that the Rum Shop. The Dry Goods

Store next to it. Up the road the High Bridge.

The Playground, founded by my father, where I spent

Many happy memories no longer there.

The land usurped by an interloper.

The bridge over the Punt Trench where

I fell into the water now collapsed, the Trench

Filled in with debris.

Across the Punt Trench and beyond,

Albouystown, the gateway to Georgetown.

A mile away and yet now so close.

10. THE HOUSE IS ALIVE

The house is alive.

An active, energetic, pulsating entity

Demanding attention.

Mangoes swollen with juice. Cannon balls

Bombarding zinc sheets. Free-falling parachutists

Jumping from an airplane.

Breeze moaning through the rafters.

Wind singing through the eaves.

Water dripping from the downspout. Ping-ping.

Floorboards creaking and shutters rattling.

Voices infiltrating through the windows,

Bouncing off the walls. A bird: *kiss, kiss, kisskadee*.

A lorry on the brick road. Walls reverberating.

A deafening trill invading my senses.

A fowl cock crowing on the rooftop.

The flickering ray of a sunbeam sneaking

Through the jalousie window. A butterfly

Caressing my cheeks.

Gliding. Swaying.

Fluttering in

A dangling pattern.

11. THE PUNT TRENCH

Memory.

Early morning rains sweeping

Away the sludge of the

Previous day. Washing the

Torpor of the night into

The Punt Trench. Fast moving torrential

Waves flashing through

The koker to the raging Atlantic.

Despair.

The Punt Trench is a dumping

Ground filled with debris and

Castoffs. Empty shell of a car.

Rusting frame of a bicycle. Bags of

Garbage piled in mounds. A dog's bloated

Carcass. Tall paragrass and wild eddo bush

Reaching to the sky.

Change.

From the koker in Public Road

All the way to the Backdam

The Punt Trench is now *Independence*
Boulevard. Every time the breeze zips
Across from the north-east.
It reeks and fills my
Nostrils. Repulsive
Odours.

Hope.
The shrill cry of a kiskadee.
The high pitched discordant
Whistle of a blue saki.
The cooing of a dove.
Life goes on!

12. COUNTRY LIFE

Under the rusted zinc sheets
Of a sprawling lumber yard planks
Are stacked on towering racks.

A man rests on the top tier.
Head propped on one hand,
Right foot crossed on his left knee.
Hands behind his head, he watches
The shadow of the mango tree creep
Remorselessly to his prostrate position.

Next door, in the bottom house
A man sways gently to and fro
In a hammock slung between wood pillars.

On the front stairs a small girl
Ensconced between her mother's legs,
A fine-tooth comb sweeping through
Long, black tresses. In the shade of
The mango tree three men play dominoes.
Bottles of beer on a small table.

If it's not done today

There's always tomorrow.

Or the day after.

13. THE REFUGEE

Fires lighting up the night sky.
Dogs barking. Cows bellowing.

I heard them long before they appeared.
The sound drifting with the unforgiving breeze
Blowing from the raging Atlantic.

Do you feel the wind now?
Do you hear the crapoud and the crickets?
It was like that. They were coming.
There was nothing I could do.

They didn't care who was innocent.
Or guilty. They wanted revenge
On someone, anyone.
For wrongs done to their own kind.
In some other place and time.

Land no more than a Backdam.
Years of toil. Through all the flooding
And the drought. Property mother

Handed down to me to be passed to my son.

Why did we become targets?

Greed? Envy?

When they come what should I take?

What *could* I take? We ran across the pasture,

Long razor-grass slicing bare flesh like a scythe.

We stumbled over soft pats of cow manure.

My heart thumping like it would tear

A hole in my chest.

The women crying.

You ask if I remember?

I remember every minute of that night.

I remember it well.

14. TROPICAL NIGHT

The sun sank fast, bringing a multi-hued
Approach to night. A painter's palette
Of reds, crimsons, burgundies.
Streaks of purple softened the edges
Of the horizon and blurred the contours of the landscape.
Everything assumed mellow proportions.
A peaceful calm descended.

The old man sat in his rocking chair.
Looking at an open savanna
At the back of the house. His vision
Never wavered. Was he thinking,
The night held unseen terror?
Like back in 1964 when he and
His entire family fled in the middle
Of the night and left everything behind?

A blackout. No streetlight. Night fell suddenly,
Swiftly, as if someone had pulled
A large cloak over the road masked
In a pall of darkness. Dark clouds blanketed

The area. A full moon came out,

And when it did, streaks of light

Shimmered off the pools of water on the road.

15. MOSQUITOES

The mosquitoes came out.
I heard them before the first one
Zoomed in.

A high-pitched, angry hum
Signalled the intent for the rest
Of the evening.

I swatted one on my right arm.
Another zipped straight into my left ear
With unerring accuracy.

A laser guided missile. I smacked my ear
And the noise subsided, replaced by
A ringing in my ear.

16. RAINY SEASON

Nights turned cooler.

Dark clouds sailed restlessly
Across the bright, silvery moon.
Crickets chirped ceaselessly,
Calling out *Quick-Quick, Quick-Quick.*

Legions of crapoud croaked interminably,
A bellowing, pulsating cacophony
Reverberating throughout the night.
Swarms of candle-flies fluttered
Through the darkness in the Backdam.

*

It started with lightning.
Not broken strings of jagged forks
Arcing across the dark sky leaving
Flashes of luminescence in their wake.

But bright bursts lighting

Up the entire sky from the Demerara

To the Backdam, from the Atlantic to

The cane fields of Ruimveldt.

Blinding light suspending

Images for disquieting interludes.

A passing cyclist hurrying home.

A whimpering dog tied under a tree.

Deafening clangs of thunder

Split the air. Pitter-patter on the leaves.

Drumming on the zinc sheets.

The roar of the wind crashing

Branches together.

The rainy season had finally started.

17. TROPICAL RAIN

Drizzles turn into a torrential downpour.

Beats on the zinc sheets, cascades

Off the roof. Rockets through the downspout

Into the steel barrel.

Like the sound of approaching rioters

The noise swells to a crescendo.

I hear the cries of the downtrodden.

The oppressed, the exploited.

Long after the rain stops the drops linger.

Ping-ping, drip-drip.

The cries remain.

18. AFTERMATH

The rain had stopped.

Nimbus clouds hung around,
Threatening.

A brisk breeze brought scents.

The uninviting odour of decay
From the stagnant water
Of the Punt Trench.

The pungent hint of citrus
From the orange tree in the front yard.
The unwelcome intrusion of the earthy
Smell of cow dung where cattle grazed.

A woman passed on the road.
Negotiated her way around the pools
Of water, a blue parasol opened up.
Bright red dress fluttering.
Long boots caked with mud.

In the gutter a pregnant pig,
Head sloughing around the bend
In the road. A goat in the neighbour's
Yard poked his way through an opening
In the fence, his progress hindered by a
Wooden triangle around his neck.

19. THE ANTS NEST

The Old Man rose from his rocking chair.

Walking over to the door
He reached up and disrupted
The flow of black ants traversing
Up and down the doorjamb.

The ants scattered in all directions.

He pointed to the orange tree.
They come from there. They working
On the ground floor, soon bring the whole house
Crashing down. That's the way. Piece by piece,

They strip everything and cart it away.

This country going the same way.
Corrupt politicians looking
Out for themselves. They all a selfish
And greedy bunch who want more and more.

The Old Man returned to his rocking chair.

The ants resumed their upward
And downward trajectory
On the doorjamb. As if nothing
Had happened.

20. LAW AND ORDER

Wherever there was a crowd of people,
The man called *Law and Order* preached
His sermon of hell and damnation for all those
Who followed a path of crime.
His cry: Repent Ye or face the wrath of God
Heard loud and clear throughout Georgetown.

His small pushcart rigged with a gallows
And trap door. A mannequin, dressed in prison
Stripes with a noose around its neck.
A Cat O'Nine Tails completed his paraphernalia.

"Repent, before it's too late," Law And Order shouts.
He whacks the mannequin with the whip and
Continues his tirade against offenders.
"If you don' obey the law, you will be punished."
Whack, whack. "Dis is what in store for you if you go to
jail."

The crowd roars: "Give him more, give him more."
Law And Order with a mouthful of crooked teeth:
"The law must be obeyed. If you do the crime,
You mus' do de time. What
Should we do with dis criminal?"

"Hang him, hang him," came the cry.
Law And Order waved his hand for silence.
The crowd was stilled. He took a lever in his hand
And pulled it, setting in motion the springing of the trap
door.

The criminal mannequin fell

And dangled by the neck.
The crowd clapped and whistled.

21. THE INDENTURED

They were Cane cutters.
Bundlers. Porters. Working for
The white overseer and local straw bosses
And the absentee English
Massa.

The contract not worth the paper
Written on by the white
Plantocracy.

Deductions:
Transportation around the sugar estate.
Buying from the company store.
Living in a one-room
Logie.

Fines:
For a sick day.
Arriving late in the field.
Straying too far from the
Sugar Estate.

Transgressions:
All kinds imagined and concocted
Prevented them from returning to their
Motherland.

Justice:
Through it all only one man
Fighting to reverse the rulings in the

White man's court. Agent Crosby the
Englishman.

And then one day, Crosby was no more.

22. MATAV

The candles had shrunk
During the night. Darkness concentrated
Around them. Large patches in which gruesome
Creatures took shape.

An oil lamp, the flame flickering
And wavering from a draft
Through the door. Ghostly images
Bouncing on the wall.
Mirages of her, of me, of my mother.

To return to the road,
We had to traverse a dark passage,
The ground unevenly covered
With a layer of coconut shells
Split down the middle.

In the rainy season those shells
Would float away…as she
Eventually did.

23. THE CROSBY PAPER

Just a child.
She came with her mother.
Brought far across the Atlantic
To a land called British Guiana.

Just a child.
But old enough to wield a cutlass.
Weed the tall razor grass.
Cut the cane stalk. Bundle it. Port it.
Load the punt. Watch the man weigh
And tally the bundles.

They told her she would return to
Mother India after five years.
Five years turned to ten.
Ten rolled into fifteen.

She's now into her ninth decade.
Eight of them in this foreign land.
She carries a slip of paper. Nestled
In her bosom. Her Crosby Paper

Tells who she is. When she came.

How Long she came for.

But it's only a piece of paper.

It's too late.

She's still here.

And this land is still not her land.

24. SOMARIA

She came by train.
We called her *Train Mie*.
A visit meant gifts for each of her grandchildren.

When she arrived and opened the cloth bag
With the polished wood handles
And faded printed flowers, six pairs of eyes
Peered into it with high expectation:
Kids eagerly awaiting the opening of gifts
On Christmas morning.

She sat in the old wooden rocking chair
As it creaked and groaned every time
She moved around, then she reached
Over to the side table for the small can
Of tobacco, a box of matches and
Cigarette paper.

She took several pinches of the tobacco
And formed a ridge in the middle of the paper,
Flicked her tongue and licked the edge

Then sealed it around the tobacco. As the cigarette

Dangled from her lips, she painstakingly

Extracted a match from the small box.

When she struck the match a tantalizing

Burst of sulphur floated across to my nostrils.

Grandmother filled her lungs with smoke,

Flicked the ashes into an empty matchbox and

Held us in suspense as she slowly

Plucked a loose strand of tobacco from her lips.

The stories she told made the hair

At the back of my neck stand on end.

25. TRAIN MAI

Spirits roaming the countryside.

Bacoo, the African spectre kept in a bottle

By the Obeahman who summoned

It to carry out his evil deeds.

Ol'Higue, the bloodsucking

Old woman roaming village to village

Looking for little boys and girls.

Moongazer, out on a full-moon

Looking for travellers foolish enough

To be out on the road at midnight.

Flying Dutchmen –spirits

Of Dutch overseers and plantation owners.

Restless souls roaming around old haunts

At night, riding white steeds, the horses

Snorting and panting to the steady beat

Of slaves chanting in the background.

Train Mie paused and took another

Drag of her cigarette. Her mother

Witnessed these phenomena and she
Too had seen many things when she
Was a little girl.

On the wall, just over her head a lizard
Paused, its light grey skin blending
With the wall, four legs outstretched.

Bulging eyes followed the insects
As they buzzed around the dim light of
The kerosene lamp casting a halo over
Train Mie's head.

The lizard's long tongue flicked out
And snatched a paper moth
From the group circling around the lamp.

I swallowed hard and moved closer
To my older brother.

26. THE PHOTOGRAPH

An image flashes across my screen saver,
Lingers for a moment, moves on.
My father.

Long gone.
So many years. His memory
Revitalized in a photograph.

He's in his mid-forties in this black and white
And it *is* the mid-forties. The year I was born.
One of two.

He's at work.
Dressed in a white shirt, striped tie, pince-nez,
Black hair. A day's stubble on his face.

He's looking down at something on his desk.
A half-smile. He seems to be happy. If he is,
It's a strange happiness.

Perhaps because of news

Just received. A disquieting mixture.

One has survived. The other, stillborn.

27. COLONIAL MENTALITY

What's all this nonsense
about independence?
These people can't rule themselves
and they want freedom?
God save the Queen!

***

Now, look what independence
bring us today.

Line up everywhere.
To buy a loaf of bread.
To make a phone call.
To buy kerosene oil to cook.

Can't walk the streets.
Choke and Rob rampant.
Thief man bruck down door
To rob and murder you.

Buildings collapsing.

Roads with holes the size of craters.

Water from the tap rusty.

Blackout every night.

Brownout during the day.

Teachers not paid.

Civil Servants on strike.

Corruption rampant.

Long line up every day outside

Canadian and US embassy for visa.

People so desperate to leave

They backtracking.

Things so much better

When the queen rule.

God save the Queen!

28. DEATH COMES IN THE END

Looking down, at my father,
I was seeing a stranger. His features
Had changed drastically. His cheeks
Were puffed and inflated by jowls,
Forehead much farther back on his head,
Nose contorted at the base. Was this the same
Man I once called Father?

So, this is what it comes down to at the end
Of your life! A man is brought up with values
Instilled in him by his family, he educates
Himself, builds a career and business,
Raises his own family, makes his name
In a community, but in the final analyses,
It all comes to nothing.

Thirty paces separated me from my father.
I crossed them in a few seconds.
The gap finally bridged.
Was it only because one of us
Now immobile, unmovable, and passive?

29. THE CEMETERY

Here was my father being placed

Next to his mother and her mother

Before her. Among people whose origins

Started in a far-off place

Across the ocean.

People who had found themselves

In a corner of the globe that would

Not have featured in their

Future plans before they were forced to

Seek their fortune.

All the others buried here.

Headstones marking their final

Resting place: a British soldier

Who died of malaria in 1920,

Far from his home.

Blacks brought as slaves from Africa.

East Indians and Chinese bonded as Indentureds

All now lying side by side. The Great Equalizer.

Rulers and conquered.

Masters and labourers.

30. MARKERS

All these graves and tombs,

Obelisks, crypts, vaults, mausoleums

And monuments.

Nothing left of life

But a token

Of a brief existence in time.

Are they remembered

For the good done in life

Or for evil deeds?

Who remembers?

Relatives? Friends? Enemies?

Lovers?

Or have they been forgotten?

The memory consigned

To photographs, objects, memorabilia.

To letters written.

Incidents and accidents of long ago.

Faded episodes in history…

31. THE GRAVEDIGGER

The funeral was over.

He scooped the earth with his shovel,
Threw it on the casket, paused,
Scooped. Threw it on the casket.
Puffs of smoke rising from the cigarette
Dangling between his lips.

How many graves had he done for the day?

The cigarette was down to a stub
By the time the last of the dirt was in
The grave but he would not let go.
He dragged out the last puffs from
The stub between his thumb and index finger

Before he tossed it on the ground.

He was a thin man, his back stooped,
Clothes hanging by threads on his
Emaciated body, face grizzled and grey,

Looking for all the world like someone

With time on his side.

Why should he hurry? Who would complain?

He took his time, tamped the mound,

Stood back and looked at his handiwork,

Twisting his head right and left, checking

Its symmetry. Then, he placed his

Shovel over his shoulder.

Slowly, he made his way out the grounds.

32. IN THE END

In the end, life is for the living.
The dead already had their place
In the sun. Once they've moved on,
A plot awaits somewhere, someplace.

In the end, this is what a man's life
Finally comes down to: Ownership
Of a six feet deep plot of land
Marked by a headstone commemorating
His coming and going.

In the end people will watch the final
Moments with the same fascination
That seem to imply there is
Some deeper meaning to the entire
Process of filling a hole with dirt
Excavated hours previously.

In the end, some will gaze
And wonder: There but for the
Grace of God, go I.

Will my turn come later
Rather than sooner?

In the end, a dome would be cast
And a headstone installed. Your name
inscribed with words that mean
Something to someone, other than you.
Died as he lived. No more, No less.

33. ECHOES IN MY MIND

The fowl-cock below my window
Broke the hallowed silence
Of the night. Proclaimed the dawn.
Disturbed the quietude
Of the tranquil neighbourhood.

Long after my return
From the land of my birth
Echoes from my childhood
Chime in my mind.

*

Echoes that stir memories of playing
In the yard. The relentless sound
Of my mother whacking
The clothes with a beater.

Left to my own devices.

Waiting for older siblings

From school. Father to return from work.

The fowl-cock squawking,

His cacophonous outcry

Creating an uproar.

A bark in the Backdam.

Followed by the tumult

Of another in the distance.

Yet another close by.

*

Those echoes rang in my ears.

Haunting every waking moment

Long after my return.

34. THE STELLING

Hucksters hawking goods.
Women with straw baskets
Loaded with brown tamarind,
Yellow mango, five-finger and golden-apple.
Hands of Banana dangling from a pole.
A man selling Vimto and I-Cee soft drinks.

Shoeless boy peddling potato balls and
Channa in paper cones.
A cane-juice vendor,
Cart parked on the parapet,
Passing long stalks of cane
Into the grinder,
Extracting the sweet nectar.
People perspiring
In the hot sun.

The ferry to Adventure has docked.
There is no queue. Just a jumble of
Perspiring bodies clamouring,
Pushing, shoving, on the gangway.
Cars creeping across the ramp to the lower deck.
A herd being ushered on the ramp. A hot, roiling
Excavation of green excrete splatters the queue.
People scatter in all directions.

35. MEMORY

Deep within the recesses
Of my mind
Hidden behind a locked
Door is your name.

Pardon me if I can't
Find the key.

My mind is already cluttered—
So many doors.
So many locks.
So many keys.

These doors hold
The way to many memories.

Some of them are faded
Over time. Some return
To haunt me. Some linger
As tattered images.

I recall your face, though.
Somewhere back when.

It jumps out. Takes me to
A time when I was young and filled
With hope. For the world. For life.
For humanity.

It's one filled with character,
Your face. I never forget a face.

I'm sure somewhere, somehow
You made an impression. It's my saving grace.
The ability to recall a face.
But pardon me if I can't remember your name.

36. DON'T CRY FOR ME

Don't cry for me
When I'm gone.

I may not be here
But you will feel my presence
In every photograph. In every journal
I've written. In every book
I've published.

Don't mourn for me
When I'm gone. I may not be here
But you can see me
In your children's faces.
In their every move and gesture.
In the faces of my siblings who survive me.
In them you will know
I was once here and not forgotten.

Don't lay me down to rest
In the cold earth.
Scatter my ashes in the sea

To be taken to all corners

Of the globe. Places I visited.

Countries I longed to go.

To the country of my birth

Where my ancestors are buried.

Don't lay a headstone

To mark my passing. I will not know.

I will not care. And in the course

Of time neither will you.

It will lie there like all

Other markers. People buried.

Long forgotten. A passing

Memory in time.

Tilted, sunken, decrepit headstones.

Don't cry for me

When I'm gone. Celebrate my life.

Play the music I love.

Read a poem I've written.

Your favourite passage

From a book I wrote.

Tell my friends and family

I lived a good life. I hope I left them

Treasured memories of their time

With me. As good as the ones of them
I will take with me.

If there is life hereafter
I will meet them. And I will meet you,
Too, someday.

37. FRAGMENTS

DISINTEGRATION OF A CITY

Places and buildings jarred my memory.

How the city had changed!

Once known as the Garden City

Of the Caribbean.

Signs of decay. Trenches filled with

Stagnant water. Garbage and tall reeds

Lined the banks. Buildings weather-beaten.

Streets perforated with potholes.

Sidewalks rutted and cracked.

HOPEFUL

Growing up in British Guiana.

A child reluctant to go to school,

Hoping it would rain so hard,

One of those long non-stop rainfalls

Resulting in floods and cancellation

Of school.

INSTANT FLASHBACK

I was going through my locker

Selecting an old shirt to do yard work.

I had an instant flash-back to

My father.

I was a child once again,

Snuggling up to my father,

Gaining comfort from his smell.

Tears started to flow.

LEARNING

I showed her how to unbolt the pantry door.

Watched as it opened a whole new world

Of things she'd never seen and held before:

Containers and packages, plastic wrapping, jars and boxes.

Adults should be like that, I thought.

Every day a new door opened to a different cupboard.

MEMORY

Forgetting what you started out to do.

Retracing your steps to trigger the memory but

It continues to elude. You're not sure how important

It was. Does it mean there might be something wrong with you?

MIRAGE

Waves of heated air shimmering

Up from the pitch on the road,

Destroying all perspective

On a hot summer's day.

NOSTALGIC

Immigrants.

As they grow older, the yearning

For a return to the old country increases.

Memories plague them, of a childhood in a familiar spot.

Any little incident will send their senses reeling and take them back in time and place.

PERSPECTIVE

In childhood time and distance

Assume massive proportions in scale.

When you return to old haunts as an adult,

You wonder how it is that you once thought it was so awesome.

SOLITARY

Trees wrapped in burlap bags

In winter. Lone sentinels.

Clothing braced against

The bitter cold, swaying, quivering,

Moaning, the wind coming through

Holes in the bags.

SURVIVAL

When I hear about the sad passing

Of a much younger man, I think

With awe and appreciation

I'm not doing so badly:

I have survived

To this age!

TRANSITORY

An overcast sky.

We passed a long stretch of open farmland,
A farmhouse set back far from the road.
The sky opened up. Rays of sunlight filtered
Through, silhouetting the building.

A rainbow appeared. The dawn of creation.
I pulled over. Reached for my camera,
Turned back. The scene had altered.

WHAT GOOD?

What good is a story if no one reads it
A song of no one sings it
A house if no one lives in it?
Are you really kind if no one feels it,

Generous if no one benefits,

Happy if no one shares it?

YOU CAN NEVER GO BACK

Sometimes I recall growing up

Back in Middle Road, the idyllic setting

Of the suburb, longing for the time again,

Knowing that it's long gone and the people

There no longer the same.

You can never go back.

ABOUT THE AUTHOR

Ken Puddicombe

Ken Puddicombe is a professional Accountant who provided controllership for a number of companies in the private sector before he retired to pursue his love of writing. His writing has appeared in newspapers and literary journals in Canada and the U.K. Originally from British Guiana [now Guyana] in South America, he immigrated to Canada and still lives there with his family. *Racing With The Rain*, his first novel was released in 2012. His second novel *Junta* was released in 2014. A collection of short stories entitled *Down Independence Boulevard* was released in 2017. This is his first book of poetry. His genre is fiction, based on international locations but especially focused in Canada, the Caribbean and Guyana. His website: http://www.kenpuddicombe.ca

ALSO FROM MIDDLEROAD PUBLISHERS

www.middleroadpublishers.ca

ALL BOOKS AVAILABLE AT AMAZON.

eBook versions available from all eBook channels

Racing With The Rain

By Ken Puddicombe

Available on amazon.com

"Ken Puddicombe's brilliant novel…an historic political conflict in Guyana, during the Cold War and the cold cynicism and tragic irony of a state sacrificed to super-power hegemony." -Frank Birbalsingh, author of *Novels and The Nation: Essays in Canadian Literature.*

"A gritty look at the politics of a nation and within a family that drive a young man from his home and from his country." -Karen Fenech, author of *GONE*

".The characters come alive in...creating enough tension to want the reader to thirst for more. As a fellow author I am impressed with this author's writing style." –Enrico Downer, author of *There Once Was a Little England.*

JUNTA

By Ken Puddicombe

Available on Amazon

"Another suspenseful tale of churning political chaos…—Frank Birbalsingh, author of *Novels and The Nation: Essays in Canadian Literature.*

"Keenly insightful of general human nature under duress, portraying both the purer and darker desires of a mixed bag of empathetic characters." —Margaret Sisu, author of *Nathaniel Myer.*

"A gripping story (of) an imperfect democracy…the tension…builds increasingly from page to page."—Rico Downer, author of *There Once Was a Little England.*

Down Independence
Boulevard And Other Stories

by Ken Puddicombe

Available on Amazon

"A brilliant collection of stories telling the tales of people forced to leave their homes…craving the past, escaping from racial conflicts and dictatorship…"—Judith Kopacsi Gelberger, author of *Heroes Don't Cry.*

"The author treats us to a collection of short stories from the tumultuous birth of a nation to the children of independence…"—Rico Downer, author of His Father's Footsteps.

"Packed with a variety of observation, richness of detail, with and humour…stories that catch the temper of a time of transition from the post-colonial Caribbean to an uncertain future." —Frank Birbalsingh, Professor Emeritus, York U.

Perfect Execution

by Michael Joll.

Available on Amazon.

"Michael Joll is a master of surprise endings, but they never seem forced. He always stays true to his characters and their worlds." —Nancy Kay Clark, author and editor, *CommuterLit.com*

"A delicious collection of short stories. These tales of love, desire, and betrayal crisscross the Atlantic, dally in Monte Carlo, and see action in the Second World War. At times funny, naugty and touching…something for everyone." Brian Henry, author, editor, blogger of *Quick Brown Fox*, and Ryerson University writing teacher.

"A must-read for lovers of classic detective murder-mystery stories…combining story-telling in the tradition of Arthur Conan Doyle and Agatha Christie, with exotic Southeast Asia locales and the mindsets of their early twentieth century British Administrators." —Raymond Holmes, author of *Witnesses and Other Short Stories*.

"As a poet, I most enjoyed the metaphors and imagery in Joll's stores…" —Debbie Okun Hill

"Exotic and intriguing! Joll brilliantly captures the reader's interest with vivid imagery and a relentless sleuth." —Phyllis Humby, short story writer, poet and novelist.

"Witnesses…immerses the reader into lives containing what can and can't be explained… Suspenseful, historical, futuristic and riveting. Holmes creates stories and characters who will stay with you long after the last page has been turned." —Bruce A. Hanson, Award winning author of adult and children's short fiction.

"Raymond Holmes' debut collection of a dozen short stories effortlessly conjures up images of people and places, real and imagined…full of unexpected twists and turns." — Michael Joll, author of *Perfect Execution And Other Stories*.

"Whether comedic or tragic, plunge his readers into vivid slightly askew worlds, where violins hold memories, suitcases vanish, ghosts abound and death waits behind every door."—Nancy Kay Clark, author of *The Prince of Sudland: Escape from the Palace*.